Farzana's Journey
A Bangladesh story of the water, land, and people

By Chelsea Peters

Illustrated by Chip Boles, Marcelle Coronel, Matt Machado, Linda J. Peters, Ayo Sanusi, and Marguerite Zabriskie

We dedicate this book to all the women and girls who have to walk to fetch their water each and every day to provide for their families, and to the polder residents, who show incredible generosity, curiosity, and joy in life.

Copyright © 2017 by Chelsea Peters
ISBN: 978-0-9992786-0-4

Illustrations by Chip Boles, Marcelle Coronel, Matthew Machado, Linda J. Peters, Ayo Sanusi, and Marguerite Zabriskie

Layout and design by Lauren Howell Anderson

Published by IngramSpark

All rights reserved. No parts of this publication may be reproduced, stored in a retrieval system, or transmitted in any form or by any means, electronic, mechanical, photocopying, recording, or otherwise, without the prior written permission of the copyright owner.

This book was prepared through the Bangladesh project of the Vanderbilt Institute for Energy and Environment at the Vanderbilt University. The author, Chelsea Peters, was a graduate student involved in research through the Civil and Environmental Engineering department and Earth and the Environmental Sciences.

Support for the book was provided by the National Science Foundation Graduate Research Fellowship, Office of Naval Research, and Vanderbilt University funding through the Curb Center, the Civil and Environmental Engineering department, and the Earth and Environmental Sciences department.

We would like to acknowledge the hard work and dedication of many Vanderbilt researchers, artists, and reviewers who were instrumental in rewriting, adapting, and illustrating the story. This book includes illustrations contributed by multiple talented artists from Tennessee and Mississippi, who diligently portrayed scientific and cultural accuracy in their artwork. The author and illustrators would like to thank the following organizations, schools, and individuals for participating in the preparation of this book:

Vanderbilt Curb Center for Art, Enterprise & Public Policy
Vanderbilt Institute for Energy and Environment
Vanderbilt Civil and Environmental Engineering
Vanderbilt Earth and Environmental Sciences
Dhaka University
Sanjana Zerin
Saddam Hossain
Ratna Rahima
Rachel Gould
J.T. Winders
Kelly Shaw
Christopher Tasich

Under the warm afternoon sun, Farzana stopped in the shade of a coconut tree to cool off. The path she needed to travel stretched as far as she could see. It was covered in slick mud from the recent monsoon rains. Looking at the flooded rice fields and the rushing tidal channel, Farzana frowned.

Suddenly a kingfisher swooped down from the tree and landed near the empty jar she had been carrying.

"Hi, my name is Tuni. Why do you look so sad?" asked the colorful bird.

Farzana said, "I'm headed to the pond sand filter in the next village. Each day I make this long walk to fetch water for my family. I don't understand why I need to walk so far when the world looks like it is covered in water."

Tuni gave her a thoughtful look. "Can I join you on your walk? I can tell you a story about your people and this land that may answer your question."

Curious, Farzana picked up her water jar and the two started down the path atop the embankment wall. "It is said," the wise bird began, "that your ancestors settled here in Bangladesh because it was the most fertile area in all the land! As snow from the Himalayan mountains melted, the water formed huge rivers that flowed south across Bangladesh."

"We call those the Ganges, Brahmaputra, and Meghna rivers!" exclaimed Farzana.

"Yes!" Tuni grinned at her. "If only you could see the rivers from my point of view!" Tuni took off and soared high above Farzana, shouting down to her, "The rivers are connected, forming the largest delta in the world! Eventually the rivers weave through these tidal channels and empty into the Bay of Bengal."

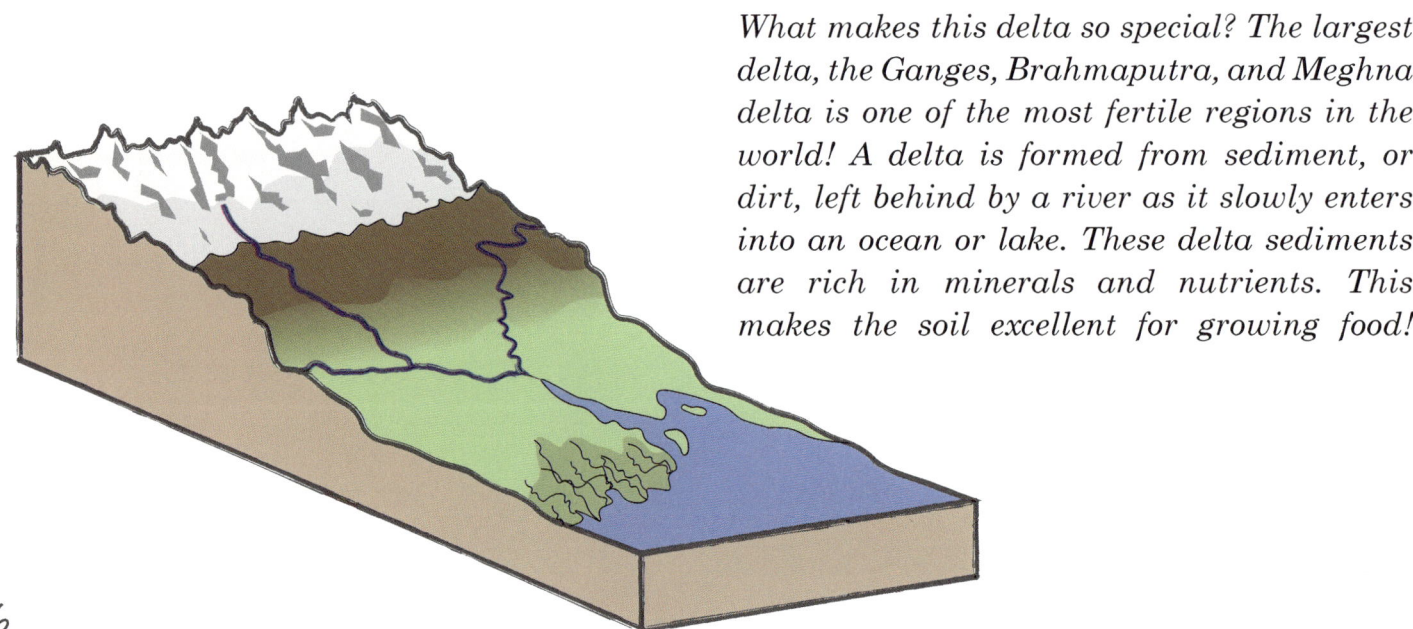

What makes this delta so special? The largest delta, the Ganges, Brahmaputra, and Meghna delta is one of the most fertile regions in the world! A delta is formed from sediment, or dirt, left behind by a river as it slowly enters into an ocean or lake. These delta sediments are rich in minerals and nutrients. This makes the soil excellent for growing food!

Farzana looked at the tidal channel thoughtfully. She had never imagined her home connected to lands so far away. Farzana knew, however, how very important the tidal channel was to her family. "This tidal channel provides the water we use to grow our rice," said Farzana, looking at the green fields. She would have to help her family harvest the crop in a few weeks.

"Yes," Tuni agreed. "Like the tidal channels, the rivers were always overflowing and this frequent flooding enabled your ancestors to first grow rice paddy. The massive amounts of water also made life difficult," continued Tuni. "The same flooding rivers that brought life to the paddy also destroyed homes and villages. So, generations of people learned to depend on and adapt to the changing rivers."

Seeing Farzana's confused expression, Tuni continued, "The rivers move slowly back and forth across the delta, carving out new channels and washing away old ones." Tuni swept his wing back and forth to show the pattern of the rivers. Skeptical, Farzana interrupted, "I've never seen the rivers moving like a snake!"

"Snake! Where is the snake?!" cried a voice from below. At that moment, a crab popped his head out of the mud and dashed to hide behind Farzana.

Giggling, Farzana scooped up the crab, while Tuni laughed, saying, "Don't worry! We were only talking about the rivers."

With a sigh of relief, the embarrassed crab introduced himself, "I'm Lalu and this bank is my home."

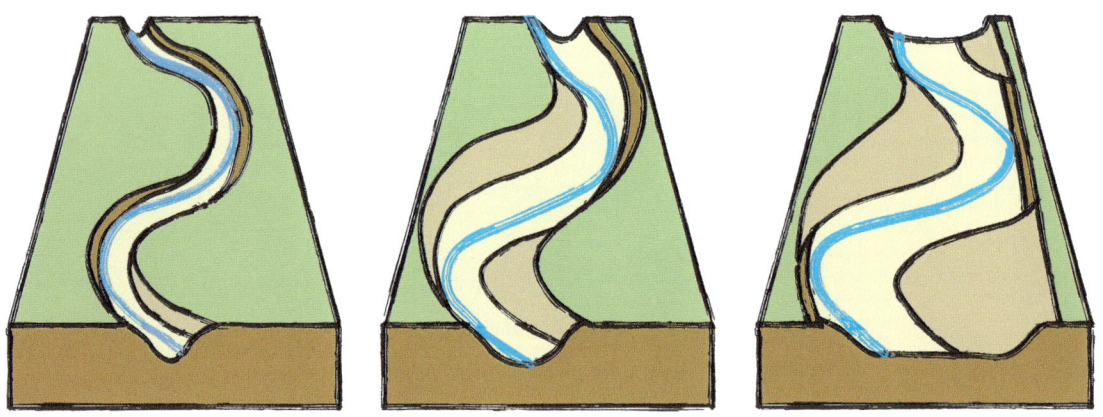

How do rivers move? Over time the river erodes, or cuts away, the bank on one side of the river channel. At the same time, the sediment that has eroded builds up on the opposite bank. These paired patterns create the side-to-side movement of river migration.

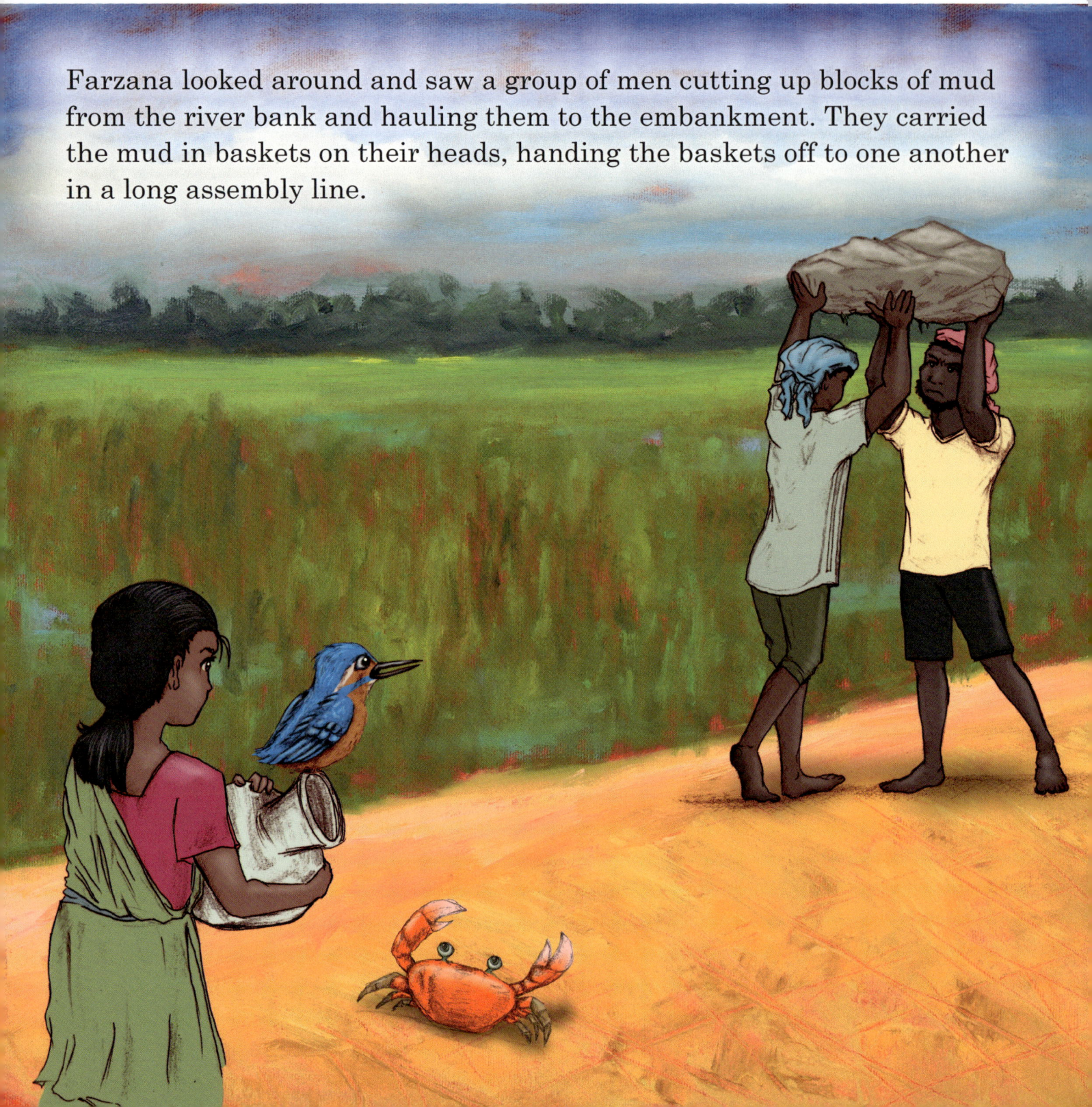

Farzana looked around and saw a group of men cutting up blocks of mud from the river bank and hauling them to the embankment. They carried the mud in baskets on their heads, handing the baskets off to one another in a long assembly line.

Looking at the crumbling embankment, Farzana guessed, "This is a spot where the villagers can't control the river!"

"Exactly!" said Lalu. "Here you see the river carving away this embankment as it moves. To stop the moving rivers, your ancestors built walls to protect the land."

Tuni added, "If you look closely you can also see the rivers moving in other ways. See? Rivers change with each tide. The rising tides bring up water from the sea to mix with the river, while the falling tide pulls the water back out to sea. The water is fresh during the rainy season, but it turns salty in the dry season." Farzana looked over to the tidal channel to see the rising water. The rushing water was chasing small crabs out of their holes and up the steep bank.

"I guess both crabs and humans play in the mud of the embankment!" Farzana laughed, setting Lalu down. After she picked up her water jar and waved at the men, the trio started down the path.

How do tides work? Tides are the rising and falling of sea levels that take place every day. This is caused by the pull of the moon's gravity on the Earth. The moon tugs on objects closest to itself, causing the oceans on opposite sides of the world to move. This swelling of the ocean water creates the high tide.

Soon the path neared a wooden dock. Farzana noticed a pair of hairy feet sticking out from under a tarp on one of the boats.

Tiptoeing over to the boat, the group peered underneath. The movement shocked a sticky macaque monkey covered in honey. The monkey rubbed her eyes from the bright sun.

"What are you doing here?" asked Farzana.

With a sneaky grin, the monkey whispered, "Men from the village were collecting honey in the forest this morning, and I snuck on their boat to have a taste. When the men returned, I was trapped! I hid from them under this tarp."

"You're a long way from home!" blurted Farzana.

The monkey scanned the horizon, where rice fields sprawled as far as she could see, and sighed, "I remember when all of this land was forest!"

"What do you mean?" asked Farzana.

The monkey explained, "All of this land was once covered in mangrove trees, but the people now use this land to live and farm. When the people developed the land, they cut down the mangroves, except for a part of the Sundarbans forest." The monkey pointed toward the mangrove forest across the channel.

Just then, the group heard the men approaching the dock. The friends scattered away from the boat. The monkey waved goodbye, slipping back underneath the tarp.

Why are the Sundarbans so important? The Sundarbans are the largest forest of salt water mangroves in the world. Mangrove trees can live in the salt water because their roots filter out the salt, giving the tree fresh water to drink. These mangroves are very important for the wildlife that live in the forest. The forest also protects coastal areas from erosion, especially during large storms.

Farzana watched the boat disappear into the distance. The monkey seemed sad about people living here now, and Farzana felt the ancient connection to the Sundarbans. But Farzana had lived her entire life on the island, so how could she know anything different? The monkey loved the Sundarbans, just as she loved her home! Her embanked island, which the community called a polder, was surrounded by over 50 other similar polders. She felt gratitude for the polders and the embankments that protected them. Although she disliked the long walk along the embankment path, she understood her life would be impossible without the walls protecting her home.

Where are the polders? These islands are located in southwestern Bangladesh, between the larger towns to the north and Sundarbans in the south.

Suddenly, a shrill squeak interrupted Farzana's thoughts. "Hey, look out! You almost stepped on me!" Farzana looked down and saw a mudskipper sitting next to one of her footprints.

Farzana asked the land-crawling fish, "Are you okay, little friend?"

"It happens all the time!" the skipper sobbed. "These embankments make my life difficult!"

Sliding across the mud, the fish propped himself up on the side of a tide pool. The mudskipper complained, "People trample my home and the embankment traffic ruins my peace and quiet. And that's not all! Ever since the embankment walls were built, water stopped spilling over into the land during the high tide. Now there are fewer tide pools for me to hide in."

"Wow! People have altered this land even more than I realized," said Farzana.

"Land and water!" corrected the mudskipper. "The water no longer carries mud to the fields, so the channels are becoming more narrow and shallow as they fill in with sediment."

As Tuni and Lalu climbed back up the embankment, Farzana paused to say goodbye to the mudskipper. "I hope that in the future we can protect my home, while also protecting yours."

As the trio approached the next village, a group of feeding cows blocked the path. A cow curiously eyed the bird, crab, and little girl.

"What an odd bunch!" the cow said. "Where are you headed?"

Farzana explained her long walk to the pond sand filter and what she had learned about people's adaptions to the environment.

She ended, "But I still don't understand why we are surrounded by water yet have so little to drink."

The cow agreed, "Drinking water has always been a problem."

Chewing on the grass, the cow mumbled, "First people dug ponds to catch rainwater, but the water soon became dirtied with…."

"Manure!" cried out Tuni. Farzana turned to see the bird hopping in circles, brushing off his feet from a pile he had just tripped over.

Farzana laughed and told him to watch his step. With an embarrassed cough, the cow said, "The water was dirtied with bacteria from the livestock."

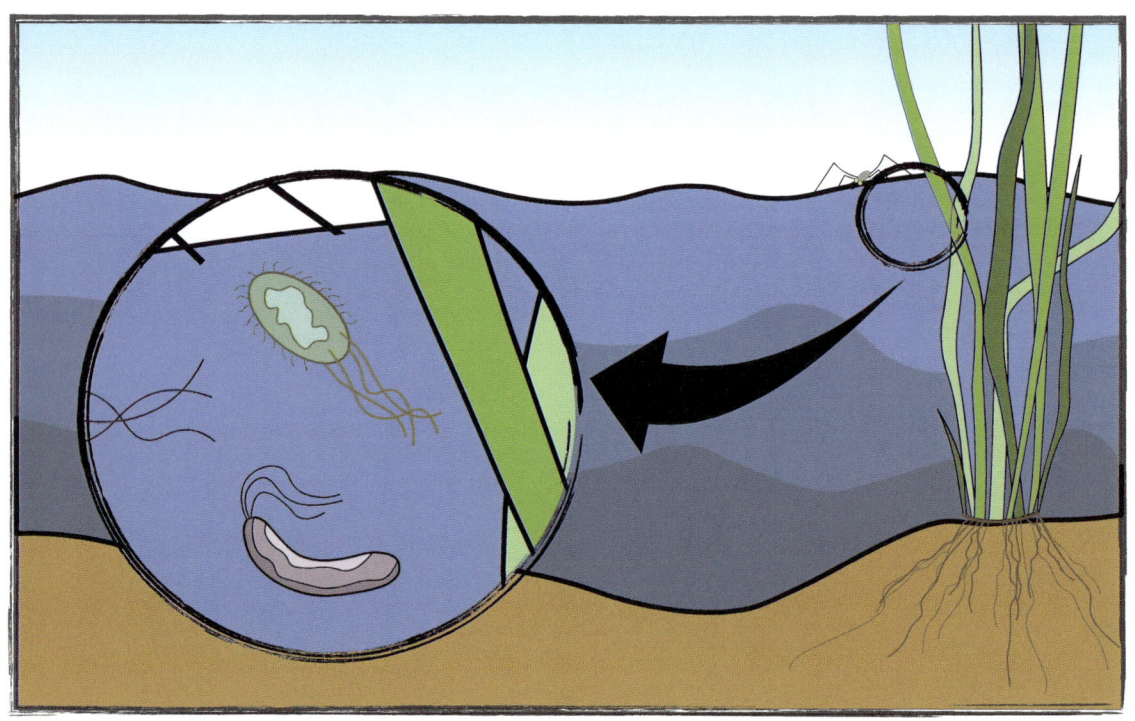

How does water make people sick? It's not the water that makes people sick, but what is in the water. Sometimes water is polluted with poop from animals or humans. The poop carries germs that can make us sick if we drink the polluted water.

"People hoped that water below the ground would be safer to drink," continued the cow.

Tuni interrupted, "Do you remember how the river moved and formed the surface of the land? Those same rivers moved grains of sediment that trapped water, called pore water. The pore water is stored underground as new sediment covers the surface, ultimately forming underground reservoirs of water called groundwater."

Lalu was busy digging a hole next to them. When he reached a certain depth, the hole began to fill with water. Lalu called out to Farzana, "Look! I found the water table, which marks the top of the groundwater!"

How does groundwater form? When it rains, water soaks into the ground and moves down through spaces between the dirt and rocks. This water is called pore water. Eventually the pore water seeps deep into the Earth and there, all the small spaces completely fill with water. The boundary between completely-filled and partially-filled pores is called the water table.

The cow continued, "The people installed wells hoping to find clean water. Unfortunately, they often found water that was too salty to drink or the water was poisoned with natural chemicals like arsenic, making humans sick."

Tuni explained, "But the people adapted by drinking rainwater and pond water instead. Households used containers to catch rainwater during the rainy season."

Farzana looked over at a nearby house. Clay jars and barrels surrounded the house to catch the water falling from the roof.

"Meanwhile, villages built pond sand filters that would clean the pond water," finished Tuni.

"No wonder I have to walk so far to get my water!" exclaimed Farzana.

"The pond sand filter is over there. I'll get back to my lunch and let you fetch your water," said the cow.

Farzana joined the line at the pond sand filter. She finally understood how drinking water depended on human adaptation to the ever-changing landscape. She thought about how the land changed and how the people had adapted. Would it always be that way? Did it mean the land would change in the future? As if reading her mind, Tuni spoke, "We will continue to see changes in the land, water, and sky. Just as your ancestors adapted, you too must overcome obstacles to live in this dynamic landscape."

How does a pond sand filter work? Pond water is added to a large tank filled with sand. As the water flows through the sand, the sand catches dirt and germs in the water. Just like any filter, the pond sand filter removes unwanted substances, making the water clean enough for drinking.

Lalu climbed to the top of the tank and nodded. "As people transform the Earth, the climate changes. You may see differences in the monsoon and stronger cyclones."

"I can help build cyclone shelters and educate my family and friends about these dangers!" Farzana assured him.

How does a cyclone form? The warm ocean water heats the air above it, causing it to rise and form clouds. Cooler air replaces the warm air, but it will also heat up and rise. As this cycle repeats, huge storm clouds form that begin to spin around a center point, called the eye.

Lalu continued, "Those storms may also flood the polder. Because the embankments prevent new rivers from adding sediment to the inside of the polder, the polder inside the embankment wall is too low and floods easily. This happens because the sediments are compacted, or packed down, over time."

How can communities prepare for flooding? After cyclones, polders can flood. When this happens, people can temporarily open embankments to allow water to move freely between the inside of the polder and the river channel. The moving water carries the sediment from the river to the polder inside the embankment. This new sediment builds up the height of the polder land. Afterwards, the embankment can be rebuilt and rice paddy can be planted again.

Farzana looked over her shoulder to see the difference between the height of the ground inside and outside the embankment. "I have heard that some communities have opened the embankments to allow water and sediment into the polder. The new sediment has restored the land to the natural height. We can adapt too!"

With each pump, the water trickled into her jar. As she finally finished pumping, Farzana reflected on the challenges her community had faced. She knew that she would play a role in helping provide water for her community. She was proud that her ancestors had come such a long way, and she was ready to make a difference in the future.

"Tuni, you are right! My life and this land are connected. Change can be difficult, but this ever-changing land is what makes my home so special."

Farzana smiled at her new friends and said, "Let's head back." The three friends set off down the dirt path toward home.

Photo by Saddam Hossain

About the Author...

Chelsea Peters, second from right, is a PhD candidate in Environmental Engineering at Vanderbilt University. She is a hydrologist who has conducted water research in coastal Bangladesh for several years. She has an intense love for environmental sciences, and especially enjoys teaching and community outreach. In her spare time, you can find Chelsea dreaming about travels to exotic destinations or cuddling her cat Abigail.

About the Illustrators...

Serving as art director and finishing artist, Chip Boles is an artist, illustrator, and muralist based in Nashville, TN.

Figure illustrator Marcelle Coronel is a pre-med student at Vanderbilt University, who is double majoring in Art and Medicine, Health, and Society with a minor in Chemistry. Her artworks vary from printmaking to sculptural ceramics, and she focuses on producing pieces that connects art her love for both the visual arts and sciences.

Diagram artist Matthew Machado is a student at Vanderbilt University, who works in several different mediums, including photography and video, that mainly focus on themes of environmentalism.

Landscape artist Linda J. Peters is an oil colorist and plein air painter based in Oxford, MS.

Animal illustrator Ayo Sanusi is an Economics and Art major at Vanderbilt University, who delights in artsy projects and little kids.

Colorist Marguerite Zabriskie is also a student at Vanderbilt University majoring in Art and Medicine, Health, and Society.

About the Research...

This book is motivated by the Vanderbilt Integrated Social, Environmental and Engineering Bangladesh Project (http://www.vanderbilt.edu/ISEEBangladesh/), which takes a multidisciplinary approach to investigate the coupling and coevolution of the physical and human systems in southwest Bangladesh. Studies explore water quality and resources, landscape alteration, climate change, and associated social migration. The purpose of this book is to increase local students' understanding of the natural world and to encourage pride in human adaptation to challenging environments.

VANDERBILT UNIVERSITY®

Photo by Chelsea Peters

Photo by Saddam Hossain

CPSIA information can be obtained
at www.ICGtesting.com
Printed in the USA
LVIC06n2007230817
546121LV00012B/107